Second-Grade Friends

by Miriam Cohen
Illustrated by Diane Palmisciano

La Toya Suzy Katy La Tanya Honey FRANKY

Nathan GREgORY JaCob

A
LITTLE APPLE
PAPERBACK

SCHOLASTIC INC.
New York Toronto London Auckland Sydney

To friends like Jacob

A LUCAS • EVANS BOOK

ISBN 0-590-47463-4

Text copyright © 1993 by Miriam Cohen.
Illustrations copyright © 1993 by Scholastic Inc.
All rights reserved. Published by Scholastic Inc.
APPLE PAPERBACKS is a registered trademark of Scholastic Inc.

48 47 46 45 44 43   6 7 8 9/0

Printed in the U.S.A.   40

First Scholastic printing, October 1993

·Contents·

·One·

The Real Author

A Real Author was coming to talk to second grade about how to be a writer and have imagination. Mrs. Rosebloom was going to put up their work in the hall so the Real Author could see what good writers they were.

Everybody was writing and writing, except Jacob. He put his head down on his desk, and started worrying. "In second grade you have to be much smarter than in first grade. You have to work, work,

work, every minute. I can't do all this hard work! In first grade I was happy all the time."

Franky was busy with something under his desk. He grinned at Jacob. He was folding a piece of paper so it would make a firecracker noise when he pulled it open. Franky never worried.

Gregory was writing a funny story. He stopped and poked Jacob. "Are you thinking again?" Gregory admired Jacob a lot. He was Jacob's real friend. "Why don't you start writing, Jacob? The Author is almost here," said Gregory.

Jacob touched Suzy on her back just a teeny bit with his pencil eraser. She turned around and stared at him through her new glasses. "Stop that!"

Jacob leaned over and whispered, "Hey, Nathan, you want to hear a good riddle?"

Nathan looked annoyed. "Jacob, I'm trying to work."

"I don't know why the kids don't like me as much as they used to," Jacob said to himself. "Probably they won't even come to my birthday party." Then he said to Franky, "I wish I was still in first grade."

"You're crazy!" said Franky.

The twins LaToya and LaTanya stopped writing. "The Real Author is coming, Jacob," said LaToya.

"We're going to get his autograph," said LaTanya.

"You'd better hurry, Jacob," they both said. Then they put their heads down over their papers again.

Jacob liked the yellow plastic airplanes, blue teddy bears, and red hearts holding all their little pigtails. He was counting them when he saw Suzy looking at him through her glasses. They made her eyes look very big and smart.

She shook her head. "Jacob, you're not working. It's very important for a Real Author to meet you."

"Oh, yes," said Katy. "I just love a Real Author. Once my aunt was shopping, and she saw a Real Author, and she ran after him to get his autograph. But it was somebody else who wasn't even an author."

Jacob said, "I would like to write a book. But it would take too long. Besides, I might get the writer's cramp." Mrs. Rosebloom had told them how writers' hands could pinch up from too much writing.

"Yeah, or a headache," Gregory said. "Nathan's going to have a *big* headache. Look how much he wrote!" Nathan's story already went down two pages and halfway on another.

Jacob covered up his empty paper with his hand.

Mrs. Rosebloom told him, "Why don't you try a poem?" So Jacob decided to write one. Poems could be really short. He looked up at the ceiling. He drew pencil lines between the corduroy on his pants. Finally he thought of a poem:

"I like my teacher.
She is nice
Because she isn't . . ."

It was really hard to think of what
would rhyme with "nice." Then he thought
of it — "pice."

"What is 'pice'?" LaToya and LaTanya
asked.

"I don't know, but it rhymes," Jacob
said.

Some of the kids laughed, because
"pice" sounded so funny.

"The Real Author is coming to see
your work in a few minutes," Mrs. Rosebloom told the class.

When Jacob heard Mrs. Rosebloom
say that, he quickly chewed his poem into
little pieces. Then he dropped them in the
gerbils' cage. It was all right because
gerbils have torn-up paper in the bottom
of their cages anyway.

Honey was ready to read her story to

the class. She was the biggest and round-est and strongest kid in second grade. She was also the nicest. Honey liked everyone. She always gave anybody who wanted one an extra-big cookie from her lunch.

"Class, let's all be ready to help Honey with her story," said Mrs. Rosebloom. "Remember, give your opinions in a kind way."

Honey began, "Once there was a cute little girl named Lou-Ann." (That was Honey's real name.) "She was the strongest in her whole class. But her stepmother said, 'There is a dance-ball, and you cannot go to it!' So she was crying in the kitchen. Then a fairy jumped out of the microwave and said, 'Come with me, and you will win a prize.'"

Suzy whispered very loud to Katy, "She's just copying Cinderella."

The teacher said, "Lots of fairy tales use those ideas, Suzy. And writers always put some of themselves in their stories." Then she sat down next to Honey. "Maybe you could try something that is not *quite* so much like Cinderella."

Mrs. Rosebloom turned around. "Have you written anything yet, Jacob?"

Jacob shook his head. He looked worried.

Katy told Jacob, "Once I didn't have any imagination, and I closed my eyes, and I got some."

Jacob closed his eyes.

"What do you see?" everybody wanted to know.

"I see . . . beavers," Jacob said. Once he and his dad watched a TV special about beavers, and Jacob got very interested in them. Every week he took out the same beaver book at library period.

"Beavers are boring." Franky laughed. "Jacob, you're *weird!*"

"Why don't you write about 'My Fishing Trip with My Father'?" said LaToya.

"I never went on a fishing trip with my father." Jacob would have loved to go fishing, but his father wasn't really that kind of a father.

"Well, what *do* you do with your father?" LaTanya asked.

"Sometimes we read together on the sofa. He reads his newspaper, and I read my library book."

"Well, what happens then?"

"We just read, and breathe," said Jacob.

"You should get your father to play some baseball with you," said LaTanya.

"Like ours does," said LaToya.

Jacob didn't want to mention it, but his father didn't know how to play baseball.

Honey was getting bored working on her story. She smiled at Jacob. In kindergarten, Honey used to put Jacob in the doll-buggy. "I'm the mommy, and you're the baby," she would say. It made Jacob very embarrassed.

Now, she came up behind him. "Hey,

look at this! I can pick up Jacob *and* his chair!"

"Put me down!" Jacob shouted.

Mrs. Rosebloom hurried over. "Honey! You could hurt somebody doing that! Put him down this minute!"

Honey went back to her seat and waved at Jacob. Jacob was only mad for a little while. You couldn't stay mad at Honey because she liked you even when you were mad at her.

"My story is ready," Katy said. It was about her Pinky Pony. She really did have a Pinky Pony, just like the one on TV. In the story, Pinky Pony found the rainbow with her little friends, the rabbit, and Raggedy Ann, and "they all had a delicious party."

"I wrote a space science fiction novel," Nathan told the class.

"How many pages does it have?" asked Mrs. Rosebloom.

"Ten, so far," said Nathan.

"Wonderful!" Mrs. Rosebloom said. "But we won't have time to read it out loud now. The Author will be here in just a few minutes. Finish your work quickly, class!"

"But I didn't write anything!" Jacob cried.

"Well, never mind, dear. You can hold the banner we made. It says, 'Welcome Author!' in such colorful letters."

Jacob scuffed his sneaker on the floor. He didn't answer. The teacher patted him, and hurried into the hall to put up their stories.

Jacob was almost crying. "I'm the only one with no imagination — I'll probably grow up without any imagination!"

"Don't make such a fuss," said Suzy. "You can still eat and walk around."

"Don't worry," Honey told him. "You want one of the cupcakes from my lunch?"

Jacob shook his head. "The Author

won't even know I'm here! He'll think I can't do anything!"

"We'll tell him," Gregory said. "We'll tell him you can bend your thumb way back and touch your arm. You can show him."

"Why don't you just write about something you're interested in?" LaToya and LaTanya said.

"It's too late! There's no time!" Jacob cried.

Katy ran and got Jacob's pencil and paper. Gregory and Franky sat him down at his desk, and pushed the pencil into his hand. Suddenly Jacob began to write. His ideas kept coming. He almost couldn't write them down fast enough.

"That's the way, Jacob," everybody cheered. "Come on, Jacob!"

The minute Jacob finished, Mrs. Rosebloom put up his story in the hall.

"He's coming!" Everybody ran to peek

out the door. The principal was smiling and smiling. She was walking next to the Author and telling him, "Our cafeteria was added in 1985."

"He's supposed to be bigger!" Franky said.

Suzy stared through her new glasses. "He doesn't look right."

Katy said, "He's not supposed to be so old."

Franky said, "Maybe it's not *really* him."

Little kindergarten children, in a line, waved and said, "Hi, Author!"

The Real Author began looking at second grade's stories. "This is so interesting," he said about Nathan's. "What a funny one!" he said about Gregory's. "I like the part about the fairy in the microwave," he said about Honey's story. Then he stopped in front of Jacob's paper. Jacob chewed on his jean jacket collar, he was so nervous.

"'Why Are There Beavers?'" read the Real Author. He smiled a lot and nodded while he was reading.

"He likes yours!" Gregory whispered to Jacob.

"All of these people have such good imaginations!" the Real Author said.

Gregory poked Jacob. "See, you've got imagination!"

Jacob said, "Well, maybe *sometimes* I do."

"Give yourself a pat on the back for fine work, Jacob," said Mrs. Rosebloom.

And Jacob did.

·Two·

Margarita

The next morning, Franky brought his cousin to school. "This is Margarita," he said. "She's from Puerto Rico, and she's visiting me for a week."

"We're so glad to have you with us, Margarita," said Mrs. Rosebloom.

Margarita had lots of soft brown hair, and she kept her eyes down when people talked to her.

"She's shy," Franky said. "And she only speaks a little English."

Jacob peeked at Margarita over his reading book.

"This is Jacob," Franky told her. "He is crazy about beavers." Franky made a Bugs Bunny face, so Margarita would know what a beaver was. Then he told her in Spanish, "Jacob *le encantan los castores*."

"*¡Ah, si!*" said Margarita. "Yes!"

Mrs. Rosebloom showed everybody where Puerto Rico was on the map. It was in the ocean below Florida.

"Hey! I didn't know it was way down there!" Gregory said.

"There's so much water around it." Suzy pointed to all the blue.

"That's because it is an island," Nathan told them.

"Is it nice in Puerto Rico?" the kids wanted to know.

"*¿Es lindo Puerto Rico?*" Franky asked her.

"¡*Ah, sí!*" said Margarita, smiling. "Yes!"

"Do they have Barbie dolls there?" asked Katy.

Margarita nodded, "¡Barbie dolls, *sí!*"

Then Katy whispered to Suzy, Honey, LaToya and LaTanya, "Come to the coatroom. I've got a secret to tell you." They took Margarita's hands. "You can come, too, Margarita."

Margarita looked happy to go with the girls, even though she didn't know what they were saying.

Franky went on tiptoes behind them to listen.

"I've got a boyfriend," Katy told the girls.

When Franky heard that, he laughed. "I bet he doesn't know he's your boyfriend. I bet there isn't any such a person. He's just in your imagination."

"There is too such a person! I can prove it!" cried Katy.

"Then what's his name?"

"James Elwood Smith, and he's in my Sunday school!"

"You get out of here, Franky! Stop spying on us!" LaToya and LaTanya chased Franky away.

When he was gone, Suzy said, "I might be getting a boyfriend. It's a boy who was at my cousin's birthday party."

"Ooh, did he say he wants to be your boyfriend?" Honey asked.

"No. But I can tell. You know that little basket of candies you get at a birthday party? Well, he gave me all the ones he didn't like."

Franky ran to tell the other kids about Katy's boyfriend.

"Eeyew!" The boys shouted, and they began falling down on the floor. "Boyfriend! Girlfriend! Yech!"

Jacob fell down and held his nose, and crossed his eyes, too.

"All right, all right, boys," Mrs. Rosebloom said. "Someday you'll think it's nice to have a girlfriend."

"Not me!" shouted Franky.

"Not me!" said Jacob. He pretended he was throwing up. The boys laughed so much, Jacob felt like a big success. He hoped Margarita was watching.

"Class, it's time for science. We don't want Margarita to go back to Puerto Rico and tell everyone second grade doesn't do any work! Jacob, will you give your beaver report? Jacob is our nature expert," Mrs. Rosebloom said to Margarita.

Jacob stood up. "This report is about beavers," he said in a loud voice. He was going to tell how beavers build hotels called beaver lodges. And he was going to say that beavers don't fight each other. They just say, "That's *your* stick of wood. But *this* one is mine." A beaver could even scare away a moose by slapping his tail on the water.

Then Margarita looked up at Jacob.

19

She had big soft brown eyes. Everything went down and around in Jacob's head, like the garbage disposal. "Uh," Jacob began. "Beavers are, uh, they're, umm . . . I forget."

"That's all right, dear," Mrs. Rosebloom said. "Sit down, and maybe you'll remember."

Jacob was so embarrassed. He was in such a hurry getting back to his seat, he tripped on his shoelaces and almost fell into the wastebasket.

Gregory said to Margarita, "He knows so much. That's why he can't think of it."

When it was time for gym, everybody was really excited. "We're doing flips today!" Franky cried.

Their gym teacher, Mr. Zito, was strong! He was stuffed with muscles that bunched all over him. And he had white stretch pants that held onto his feet with elastic. Everybody in second grade loved it when he said, "Hup!" and turned them right over in the air, and back on their feet again.

Mr. Zito blew his whistle. "Line up! Who's first? Okay, Franky!"

Franky hit his fists on his chest. He roared like Dino, the New Jersey Dinosaur. That was the wrestler on TV. He charged toward Mr. Zito.

"Hup!" Franky's sneakers made a happy *thwop!* as he landed.

Honey was next. Mr. Zito needed all his muscles to lift Honey and turn her over.

When it was their turn, each kid ran to Mr. Zito to get flipped.

"Ooh, it was fun!"

"It was *so* easy."

"I almost hit the ceiling!" Franky cried.

Shyly, Margarita tried. Mr. Zito only had to help her a little. Smiling, she ran back to the line.

Jacob was last. He looked down at the shiny gym floor. *Skwik, skwik,* went his sneakers. Jacob charged up to Mr. Zito — and turned around and went the other way. "Just a minute! I wasn't ready that time! In a minute I'll be ready. Just one minute!" And he ran around in a circle, hitting himself on the chest like Franky.

"Go, Jacob! You can do it!" LaToya and LaTanya called to him.

Jacob charged again. The same thing happened.

"Don't be afraid. I'll help you," Mr. Zito told him. Grabbing the back of Jacob's shorts, he flipped him before he could run the other way. "Atta boy, Jacob!" Mr. Zito said.

Jacob knew he wasn't like Franky. He wasn't Dino, the New Jersey Dinosaur. He was more like a beaver. A beaver just needed more time to build his lodge. And a beaver could scare a giant moose away just by slapping his tail. The kids in his class knew what Jacob was really like. But somebody like Margarita wouldn't. She'd just think he was weird.

They had math next. All the way up the stairs from the gymnasium, Jacob was feeling smaller and smaller. He *was* less tall than most of the kids in his class. But he always ran around a lot. That way the kids wouldn't notice so much. He was sure his friends didn't notice, but Margarita might.

Everybody rushed into their classroom. Jacob came in slowly, the last one.

"Today, we will be working on subtraction," Mrs. Rosebloom said. She was writing problems on the board. "Remember — think before you answer. Don't rush. Just relax, and you'll get it right."

"Math is so easy, it's boring," Katy said.

Jacob didn't think so. When Mrs. Rosebloom taught them about it, Jacob wondered, why is there math? And pints

23

and quarts? Who ever saw a plus? Or a minus? A beaver you could pet. Who would ever want to pet a plus?

Mrs. Rosebloom was saying, "If two boys have five apples each, and they each give away two . . ."

"Oh, boy!" Jacob knew *that* answer. It was almost exactly like a problem they had last time. "Seven" was always the answer to that kind of question. Jacob looked at Margarita and shouted, "Seven!"

"You weren't listening to what I said, Jacob. You didn't think before you answered."

Jacob got very busy fixing all the things in his pencil box. He didn't look up. He tried to stay behind Suzy, so Margarita couldn't see him.

Mrs. Rosebloom pointed to Nathan, who was working on the next problem already.

Nathan announced, "If two boys have five apples each, and give away two, they'd each have three left. You *could* make it harder by saying, 'How many would they have left all together?' That would be six, of course."

Jacob groaned.

All that week, Jacob didn't act like Jacob. He stayed by himself a lot. One morning, Honey saw him on the playground before school started. He was trying to get the basketball into the hoop. Mostly he dribbled it. Sometimes he whispered, "Hup!" and threw the ball up. But it came right down before it could go into the basket.

Honey ran and lifted Jacob and the ball high so he could reach the hoop. "I'm helping you," she told Jacob when he got upset.

He got *so* upset, he almost hollered, "Put me down, you big fat person!" But he didn't, because Honey was never mean to anybody.

Lucky for Jacob, no one was watching.

The girls showed Margarita how to jump rope and they taught her to say the jump rope rhymes. Margarita blushed when she tried to speak English.

"You speak good!" the girls told her.

Jacob stood far away and watched. He pretended he wasn't even looking at Margarita.

On Thursday, some of the kids were talking about Jacob.

"He wants to be Margarita's boyfriend," said Gregory.

But Franky said, "He'd never be crazy like that! Girlfriends are always bothering you. 'Are you Suzy's boyfriend or mine?' Yech!"

"Margarita wouldn't be Jacob's girlfriend, because you have to be popular to have a girlfriend," said LaToya.

"We mean, Jacob *is* popular," said LaTanya, "but not *that* kind of popular."

"He doesn't look like a boyfriend,"

Katy said. "I mean, I'm not saying he's little. He just looks little."

"Anyway," the kids said, "Margarita has to go back to Puerto Rico. This is almost her last day."

Friday afternoon, Franky's uncle drove his taxi to school. He had come to take Margarita's mother and grandmother and Margarita to the airport.

Everybody called as they drove away, "Good-bye, good-bye, Margarita. Come back again!"

"You can stay at my house!" the girls called.

Jacob wanted to shout, "Come back soon!" But he didn't. He watched till he couldn't see Margarita's soft brown hair in the back window of the taxi anymore.

After supper, Jacob stayed in his room by himself. He could hear Margarita all the way from Puerto Rico. She was saying, "Why is Jacob so weird?"

On the way to school Monday morning, Franky ran to catch up with Jacob. "Hey! Look what Margarita gave me to give you!" He held up a postcard with a picture of a pretty lady leaning on a palm tree. All around her was blue blue sky and green green water. The lady was smiling, just like Margarita. On the back it said:

> *"Querido Jacob,*
> *¿Cómo estás tú? Estoy bien.*
> *Tu amiga,*
> *Margarita."*

"What does it say?" Jacob asked. Franky told him:

> "Dear Jacob,
> How are you? I am fine.
> Your friend,
> Margarita."

All day Jacob kept peeking at the postcard. When he got home, he put it in his
secret treasure box under the bed, with his
reindeer's tooth, Mickey Mouse autograph
his Grandma had sent him from Disneyland, and a teeny plastic mug of root beer
that looked *so* real.

·Three·

Mrs. Rosebloom's Present

"**M**y mother said that Mrs. Rosebloom has been teaching second grade for twenty years!" Katy told the kids.

"Wow! Twenty years!" said Franky. "She needs a present."

That's why, on Saturday, the whole second grade went to the Wee Giftie Gift Shop. They were picking out an anniversary present for their teacher.

"Let's get her this!" Jacob cried.

"What is it? What's it for?" everybody asked.

"It's a belt that's got a little flashlight, and a whistle, and a can opener, and a toothbrush! It's for camping."

Nobody wanted to get that for Mrs. Rosebloom.

"Don't you want some help picking out a nice gift?" Jacob's mother and Katy's mother asked. They had brought everybody in their cars to the shopping mall.

"No!" Jacob said. "We can do it by ourselves."

So Jacob's mother told Katy's mother, "I'll keep an eye on the kids. You go and see if there's a sale at Rosie's Dress Shop. It's right across the way." And she went near the window where she could see second grade, and Katy's mother holding up dresses.

"Let's get her this card," Honey said. "It smells like a cake."

Katy sniffed. "It's supposed to be flowers."

"How about this big box of candy?"

31

somebody said excitedly.

"No," LaToya and LaTanya said. "She wouldn't want candy because candy makes ladies fat."

"Let me shake the bag," Franky said to Suzy. She was holding the paper bag with all the pennies and dimes and nickels and quarters that second grade had collected. It made a nice noise when you clinked it all together, like treasure.

"Here's something I *know* she'd like," said Jacob. "My mother has one, and she's crazy about it." He touched a big white china dish with roses on it.

Suddenly everybody got very quiet. Jacob felt a long, bony finger poking in his back. When he looked up, the store lady was staring down at him. Her eyeglasses were flashing bad thoughts about boys.

"Do you see that sign, young man?" She pointed to a card on the wall.

Jacob read, "YOU BREAK IT, YOU JUST BOUGHT IT."

"What does that mean?" Gregory asked Nathan.

"You have to buy it if you break it," Nathan whispered.

"But Mrs. Rosebloom wouldn't want a broken dish," Gregory whispered back.

"Where is your mother?" the store lady asked Jacob.

"Right over there." Jacob showed her his mother in the front of the store.

"Well, you shouldn't be in here without a grown-up watching you *every single* minute. Don't touch *anything*."

The lady folded her arms and stood where she could stare at each second-grader.

"Let's get her this teeny tea set!" said Suzy, pointing with her chin. On a doll-sized tray was a teapot, and cups and saucers that matched. It was so little and perfect, the girls couldn't believe it.

"You just want to play with it," Franky told them. "Teachers don't play." He

pointed with his elbow to a china ballet lady. "Mrs. Rosebloom can put it on her coffee table and look at it."

"Yeah!" everybody cried. "How much is it?"

"Six dollars," Jacob read the tag. "That's just what we have!"

"That's *sixty* dollars," LaToya and LaTanya told him. "If we had sixty dollars, we could buy anything in the whole New York City!"

Then Suzy saw it, in a glass case with glass shelves. It was throwing out little rainbow sparkles among the china mice and rabbits — a baby deer made out of glass.

"It's beautiful!"

"Let's get it!"

"How much is this?" Katy asked.

The store lady gave them more bad looks. "Five dollars. With tax, it's five dollars and forty-one cents."

Jacob was worried. "But we have six dollars."

Katy dumped out the money, and the lady gave her back fifty-nine cents. The little glass deer was put in a cotton bed, inside a white box, with gold stretchy string around it. Katy carried it with both hands to her mother's car, like a tiny baby.

The next morning, everybody was waiting for Katy to come. She stepped very carefully out of her car, holding the little box.

"Don't get too close!" Honey put her arms out like the crossing guard. Then the girls sat down on the playground bench. They put their hands on Katy's lap so they could touch the box, too.

"Let us see the present! Come on! It's not yours!" the boys cried. Franky reached for the box.

"Get away! You'll break it!" screamed the girls.

Franky grabbed for the box.

"Take it easy! There's gonna be a mess," LaToya and LaTanya told him. But Franky jumped around the bench, shouting, "You don't own it!"

Jacob didn't usually shout and grab, but this time he did, too. "Yeah! We want to see it! You don't own it!"

By mistake, Jacob bumped into Franky. Franky fell on top of Katy, and they both landed on the ground.

"It's broken! You broke it!" Katy cried. When she got up, she said, "I can hear it shaking around!"

Everybody stopped. They groaned when Katy pulled the lid off the little box. The tiny deer was in sparkly rainbow pieces.

"Now, see what you did, Jacob and Franky!" Katy looked at them like the Wee Giftie store lady.

"He made me! He pushed me!" Franky said, and he pushed Jacob hard.

Jacob cried, "But it was a mistake!"

Franky punched Jacob anyhow. Franky threw his arms around Jacob and squeezed, till both their faces got red. Then Franky sat on top of Jacob and bounced so hard that Jacob went "Uhf, oof!"

Jacob had tears in his eyes, but nobody could think how to make them stop. Then Honey sat down on both of them. "You could hurt yourselves," she said to Franky and Jacob. She only let them get up when they said they were through fighting. They were really glad they didn't have to be enemies anymore.

"Now," said Katy, "what are we going to do about Mrs. Rosebloom's present? If *only* Jacob didn't break our darling little deer — " she started to say.

"We could make her a card," Gregory said.

"Uh-uh. A card is too usual," Katy said.

"Wait a minute!" said Jacob. "We'll be right back." He whispered something to

Franky, and they disappeared around the side of the school. They came back dragging a giant cardboard box.

"First, we have to smash it flat," they said. Then Jacob and Franky explained what the class was going to do with it.

"Neat! We'll make the rainbow," said LaToya and LaTanya. "Nathan can do the letters. He doesn't even need a ruler."

Everybody took their crayon sets out of their knapsacks.

"*I'm* the one who does the holes!" said Franky.

"Stop working on my part, Katy!" said Suzy.

"This is going to be *so* great!" Jacob said. "Hurry up. It's almost time for school!"

Mrs. Rosebloom was at her desk, doing her reports, when she heard big, cardboard noises. She looked up. Through the door, bumping and giggling, came a long long piece of cardboard. It had lots of feet on the bottom, and hands holding on at the top. Crayon flowers and rainbows decorated it all over. Each second-grader's face showed through round holes.

"Happy twenty years' anniversary to you! Happy twenty years' anniversary to you! Happy twenty years' anniversary dear Mrs. Rosebloom, Happy twenty years' anniversary to you!"

Franky started the part ". . . You live in the zoo . . ." but Katy's elbow poked him on one side, and LaTanya's poked him on the other.

"A *live* anniversary card!" said Mrs. Rosebloom. "How unusual!" And she took out a round tin box filled with oatmeal raisin sunflower seed cookies she had baked for her class. "I was going to give *you* a surprise for my twentieth anniversary. Instead, you gave *me* one." She looked really happy.

Jacob said, "I'm going to have a birthday party in about one week. And it's going to have—"

But Katy interrupted. "Mrs. Rosebloom, we had a *much* better present. We had the cutest little glass deer we bought for you, but Jacob . . ."

Jacob put down his cookie. He looked miserable.

"Oh, I like the card much better. It

shows such imagination," Mrs. Rosebloom said, smiling at Jacob.

Every time Katy remembered and started to tell on Jacob, Franky shouted, "Hey! Listen to my duck imitation! Quaaack! Quack-quack-quack!"

Then LaToya and LaTanya sang "The Rainbow Connection," and Nathan told a riddle. Finally, Katy gave up.

Everybody was having seconds and thirds and fourths of the cookies. But Jacob and Franky had fifths!

·Four·

The Fishing Trip

Jacob sat on the porch steps. His mother and father were swinging in the porch swing. Jacob started making his dog, Toby, look like a beaver. He pulled Toby's lips back so you could see his front teeth, and held his ears down on his head.

"Jacob, don't do that to the poor dog!" his mother said.

"Well, I never get to do anything," Jacob said. "LaToya and LaTanya go fishing about every week. And Nathan's father took him out to the deep sea, and they caught a giant fish."

Jacob's father looked at Jacob's mother. Then he said, "Jacob, what would you say if I told you I was going to take you on a fishing trip? Yes sir! I'm going to borrow fishing equipment from my friend Joe Zimmerman, and we're going!"

Jacob was so happy, he jumped off of the steps and flopped over backward on the grass with his arms stretched out. "I never went on a fishing trip with my dad in my whole life! And now we're going! I can't believe it!"

In his dream that night, Jacob caught a giant fish with a big sword on its head. Margarita was there, and she took a picture of him standing next to it.

Driving along in the car, Jacob's father looked happy in his fisherman's hat, even though he wasn't really a fisherman. He liked to stay home and read.

Jacob clicked the little wheel on the rod. "This is great equipment, isn't it, Dad?" He looked in Joe Zimmerman's blue box. It had swinging-out drawers full of hooks and lines and rubber wigglers. The fish thought those were food.

They also had a camera. It was going to take pictures of Jacob and his dad holding up the big, shiny speckled fishes.

"Even the car is happy, Dad. The wheels are saying, 'Going fishing, going fishing, going fishing.' Dad, is this early enough? LaToya and LaTanya said you have to go *very* early to catch the fish."

"You bet it's early! I was fixing our breakfast at five-thirty this morning."

Jacob's father made oatmeal for their breakfast, but Jacob was too excited to eat. Then he did, because his father said, "We need strength for pulling in those fish."

"There it is!" Jacob cried. "It says, 'Manny's Fishermen's Cove.'"

Pine trees marched all around the

lake. Rowboats bumped against the shore. Other fishermen were drinking coffee and checking their equipment.

"I guess we'll need some bait," Jacob's father said to Manny.

"They've been taking some big ones with these night crawlers. Try 'em." Manny sold them a white cardboard box with wriggling spaghetti inside. It was really red worms, with lots of little black legs up and down their sides.

Manny picked out a boat for them. "This one's got a nice wide bottom. She's safe as a rocking chair. You could take your grandmother out in it."

They sat on the wooden seats. Jacob's father rowed, and the shore started leaving them.

"This boat is really strong, isn't it, Dad?"

"It sure is."

"The only thing is, the water's so wobbly," Jacob said.

The other fishermen were already plunking their bait into the lake.

"Hurry up, Dad! They'll catch all the fish!"

It was taking a long time for Jacob's father to hook a worm on the end of the fishing line. Finally he said, "I think we could use these rubber wigglers, don't you?"

Jacob said, "That's much better. Then we could just let the worms go home in the dirt after we're through fishing."

They sat quietly with their wigglers in the water. Jacob held his rod tight in case a big one came. Across the water, fishermen were reeling their reels in and slapping fish into the bottoms of their boats.

"The water must be better over there, Dad."

"Well, it's probably deeper. If there's one thing fish like, it's deep water." Jacob's father rowed them next to the other boats.

Slap!

47

"Nice one, Bill!"

Slap!

"Boy, that's a beauty! Must be three pounds, maybe four."

A big man had on a sweatshirt that said, "In Heaven the Fish Are Always Biting." He said to Jacob, "Sonny, try jerking your rod up and down. Like this. Just a little, not too much."

So Jacob and his father tried that. "Just a little, not too much," Jacob's father told him.

"Dad, is it lunchtime?"

"Well, what do you know, it sure is. Fishing *really* makes you hungry."

They took out their sandwiches. "Tuna fish, with little bits of pickle in it! Neat!" said Jacob.

They each had their own small glass bottles with cherry-apple juice, and plenty of peanut butter cookies. Jacob ate with one hand so he could hold his fishing rod with the other.

"I'll keep fishing so we won't miss any fish. Fishing takes a long time, doesn't it, Dad?"

"We just have to be patient, that's all, Jacob."

At one o'clock, Jacob asked, "What time is it, Dad?" At one-thirty, Jacob asked, "What time is it now?" At two o'clock, Jacob said, "The fish are probably taking a nap. Then they'll come up and bite, won't they, Dad?"

"I'll bet you're right," said his dad.

"I wonder if fish lie down when they sleep," Jacob said. "Maybe I could hit 'em on top of the head with this rubber wiggler."

Jacob began jangling his line all around in the water. "Wake up! Snacktime!"

His dad said, "We just have to relax and pretend we're not even trying to catch a fish. *That's* when they come."

They fished for a very long time. The

sun was going behind the pine trees, and all the other fishermen were rowing in to shore. Then Jacob knew it. There weren't going to be any pictures of Jacob and his dad holding up the big, shiny speckled fishes.

"What's the use of fishing? Fishing is dumb!" Jacob said.

But his dad said, "Wait a minute! There's something BIG on my line! Help me reel it in!"

It took a lot of strength. "Umf! Ugh! Oog!"

"It's coming! It's by the side of the boat!" Over the side and into the bottom. *Blop!*

"It's just a lot of mud and sticks," Jacob said. Then he shouted, "This equipment is rotten. You'd better tell that Joe Zimmerman not to lend us rotten equipment anymore!" Jacob was mad.

His father said, "It's a piece of a beaver dam, I think. Maybe you could take it to school and show it to your friends. Remember how interested you are in beavers?"

Jacob turned around so his back was toward his father. They rowed to shore without saying a word, but Jacob was muttering to himself. "My own father couldn't even catch a fish."

"How did ya do?" asked Manny.

"Oh, not so good. But we caught a lot of fresh air, ha! ha!" said Jacob's father. He didn't sound funny even though that was supposed to be a joke.

Jacob's dad wrapped the piece of beaver dam in some old plastic and carried it to the car with the rest of their things. Then he dumped the worms on the soft dirt under some bushes when nobody was looking.

"Well, at least the worms are happy, right, Jacob?" But Jacob wouldn't answer.

Riding in the car, Jacob still wouldn't talk. Then he sneaked a look at his father's face. It looked like Toby's when they thought he made a mistake on the rug, and it was just water.

Maybe, when he was a kid, his dad couldn't do things so well, either. Maybe he was like Gregory. Gregory wasn't very good at math, or writing, or catching a baseball. But he was a good person!

Jacob sneaked another look. The fishing hat made his dad look funny. Maybe people would even laugh if they saw him. But they'd better watch out! They'd better not laugh at *his* dad. So what if he couldn't catch a fish?

He reached for the piece of beaver dam. "Dad, did you know I'm starting a beaver museum in my room?"

"No, I didn't. That's a *really* good idea."

His dad sat up straighter.

"Dad, let's sing 'Ninety-nine Bottles of Pop on the Wall,'" said Jacob.

His dad grinned at Jacob in the seat

beside him. He puffed out his chest, and sang really loud.

They sang all the way to "No more bottles of pop on the wall."

When they got out of the car, Jacob's dad put his arm around Jacob's shoulder. Jacob put his arm around the middle of his dad. It was bumpy to walk together, because his dad was tall and Jacob was short. But they walked like that over the lawn, up the steps, and into the house.

·Five·

Why Are There Beavers?

Jacob slapped his books and his lunchbox down on his desk. "Don't forget! Don't forget!" he told his friends. "My birthday is tomorrow." Everybody started giggling. Jacob could feel his face turning red. Why was everyone laughing at him? he wondered.

Suzy stared at the kids through her glasses. "Shhh!" She put her finger on her lips. Then she said to Jacob, "What kind of presents are you going to have for the kids at your party? Don't get those little magic fairy wands for the girls. They had those at the last party I went to. I wouldn't want the same thing."

"Neither would I," Katy said.

"I hope, I pray, I don't get another pirate pencil sharpener!" said Franky.

"I wish we would get cap-shooters," a lot of the boys said. But Jacob knew his mother would *never* get those.

"For our birthday we're going to the bowling alley," said LaToya. "And the whole class is invited," said LaTanya.

"Ooh! I love bowling!" cried Franky. "It's so great! I went with my uncle, and I bowled almost 100!"

"Once I went to a birthday party, and it was in a swimming pool," said Katy. "It was lovely."

Jacob began to really worry — his party was just in his house. Nobody loved coming to a house.

Mrs. Rosebloom looked up from checking the roll. "Class, newstime is over."

She always let them start the morning telling their news to the other kids. Then they were ready to work.

"First grade is coming to our room in just a few minutes to hear our reports. It really helps them learn and get ideas when you bigger people teach the little ones.

"Suzy is going to tell about her trip to California last summer. Nathan will explain fractions. And LaToya and LaTanya will show their grandmother's family-story quilt. Jacob, are you ready to share all the nice things you know about beavers?"

"Well, I want to, but I don't know if I can do it," Jacob said. "Maybe I'll forget again." He remembered when Margarita was visiting their class.

"You could make notes on a piece of paper. Then you could look at them if you need to," said Mrs. Rosebloom. "I *know* you'll do a good job."

Jacob took out his library book about beavers to study.

"Oh, no! Beavers!" Franky laughed. All the kids began giggling again.

"Mrs. Rosebloom, I changed my mind," Jacob said.

It was too late! The first-graders were marching in. Suzy waited in front of the room to give her report. Then Franky started making piggy noises just to get her mad.

"Franky!" When Mrs. Rosebloom made her eyebrows go like that, they knew she was really mad. "Go ahead, dear." She nodded at Suzy when the first-graders were all sitting down. "Suzy is going to tell us about the state of California. She visited there this summer."

"'My Family's Trip to California,'" began Suzy.

"It was my birthday, so my family decided to take me on a trip to California. First, naturally, we went on the airplane. You get a little tray divided up, with mashed potatoes in one part, a hamburger in another part, and salad. Also dessert. That was lunch.

"Naturally, we also got a snack. And a movie if you pay two dollars.

"When we got to California, we stayed at a hotel with its own restaurant right in it. Each floor has its own soda machine, so you don't even have to go downstairs . . ."

"Uh, Suzy," interrupted Mrs. Rosebloom. "Could you tell us what California looks like? Are there interesting places to see?"

"Oh, yes. There are palm trees, which you would never have in New York. And we saw them acting in a movie, and we went to Disneyland, which has . . ."

"That was lovely, dear. . . ."

"I'm not finished. So, I recommend that you go to California for a really interesting and fun vacation."

"Thank you, Suzy. I'm sure our first-graders enjoyed your talk. Now it's Jacob's turn."

Jacob stood up, holding his notes in front of him. He opened his mouth, but no words came out. When they finally did, Jacob thought he sounded like a gerbil. "Some people say, 'Why are there beavers?' Well, they build dams so there will be a pond. Then they swim and find food in it, like lilies."

Suzy and Katy started to giggle.

"They bite down trees to make more dams, and they build beaver lodges in the dams. That's like a hotel for beavers."

Jacob looked up. Suzy and Katy were laughing so hard that they shook all over. The whole second grade was stuffing their hands into their mouths to keep from laughing.

Mrs. Rosebloom got up from her seat. She stood up *very* tall. Her eyebrows came together on her forehead. "We have little children depending on us. I cannot believe that *my* second grade would behave like this!" Everybody got really embarrassed.

"Please go on, Jacob. You are doing an *excellent* job."

"Work, work, work. They work practically all the time to keep the dirt from sliding down to the ocean. If it wasn't for beavers, the whole of America might be gone!"

A little girl in first grade began clapping. She thought Jacob's talk was finished. But Jacob was getting so excited about beavers, he didn't stop even when he dropped his notes. He forgot that the kids had laughed at him. He waved his arms and walked back and forth. The first-graders looked up at him with their mouths open.

"Beavers help each other carry logs with their teeth. Also, they have front paws that are like little hands. They never fight. If they feel like fighting, they just push each other for a while, but they don't bite. The families play with their babies, and give them rides in the water.

"So don't shoot beavers! Don't smash up their dams! Help all beavers NOW!"

"Ha! Ha! Ha!" His own class was laughing so hard, they couldn't stop.

Just then, the principal's voice came on the loudspeaker. "We will have to shorten this period because of the teachers' meeting. Please go immediately to your next class."

"Hey! Our next class is gym!" Franky cried. Everybody rushed to line up. First grade marched away with their teacher. Then a little boy came running back, crying because he forgot his toy car. Mrs. Rosebloom got down on her knees to help him look for it.

Walking in the hall, everybody in second grade was whispering about Jacob and laughing, even Honey, "Shh, shh!" went the kids when Jacob came near.

"They hate me! They think I'm boring and stupid and weird. That's why they're laughing," Jacob said to himself. "If only my birthday wasn't tomorrow! If only I didn't have to go to my own party!"

When Jacob got home from school, his mother said, "Today I bought all the party presents for your class."

"What are they?" Jacob asked.

"Well, for the girls I got those cute little fairy wands, and for the boys . . ."

"Oh, no! You got pirate pencil sharpeners!" said Jacob.

"Don't you think your friends will like those?"

"They probably won't even come," Jacob said.

"You're being silly," his mother said. "Everybody loves birthday parties. Wait till you see the special cake I ordered from the bakery! I'm not going to tell you what's on it. You'll be *so* surprised."

· Six ·

The Birthday Party

Jacob didn't want to wake up.

His mother tickled his foot that was sticking out of the covers. "Are you going to sleep all day on your birthday?"

"What's the use of getting up?" Jacob said.

"What's the use of getting up? Daddy's gone to pick up the cake. We've got to get ready for your party! Hurry up and get washed, now."

In the bathtub, Jacob talked to himself. "At least I have my mother and father.

They like me." Slowly he put on his good pants and a new red shirt with a bow tie that his grandma sent him for his birthday. He went downstairs, one step at a time.

If only his father was rich! They could take Jacob's whole class to Disneyland for his birthday party. Nobody would laugh at him then. Everybody would want to come.

"Don't come in the dining room, whatever you do, Jacob! The cake is here," his father told him.

While he was helping his mother wrap the boys' presents, Jacob said to himself, "These are stupid presents. What can you do with a pencil sharpener except sharpen pencils?"

When he was washing the carrots for carrot sticks, Jacob muttered, "Probably almost everybody in my class hates carrot sticks. They won't eat them even if they come."

Later, Jacob was dusting, while his father ran the vacuum. Jacob wondered, where does the dust come from? Why couldn't he and his dad just turn the vacuum around, and chase all the dust out of the front door, instead of saving it in a bag?

While he was imagining that funny idea, Jacob wasn't worrying. But then he began to see a movie in his head. It was his party with nobody there! Just Jacob and his mother and father sitting in front of the cake. Each of them was trying to smile so the other ones wouldn't feel bad.

An even worse picture came in his mind. All the kids came to his party. But they started saying, "Give us back the presents we brought you! This is a rotten party!" And they rushed out the door with his presents!

At a quarter to two, Jacob's mother said, "Oh, no! I forgot to pick up my pitcher for the fruit drink! I lent it to Mrs. Simpson. Jacob, will you run and get it?"

Jacob scuffled his new shoes through the dirt in the backyard. When he got through the hedges to Pine Avenue, he saw that his new pants had a snag in them from the hedges. What does it matter? thought Jacob. All the way down the block to Mrs. Simpson's house, he stopped to study the cracks in the sidewalk.

He rang the bell.

"Could we have the pitcher, Mrs. Simpson? It's for my birthday party."

"My goodness! How old are you now, Jacob?"

"Eight."

"Eight! Well, you certainly have grown up to be a wonderful boy! I know you'll have a really fine party." She kept saying things like that all the time she was looking in the dish closet for the pitcher.

"Mrs. Simpson is the only one who thinks I'm any good," Jacob said to himself. "Everybody else knows I'm really stupid and boring and weird. Pretty soon, my parents will even find out."

"It was right here all the time! If it

were a snake, it would have bitten me."

Jacob didn't believe a pitcher could bite anybody like a snake, but Mrs. Simpson was so nice, he didn't say that.

"Happy, happy birthday, Jacob!" she called after him. Jacob groaned.

Coming up the porch steps, Jacob had a strange feeling. His house always smiled, and winked its window-eyes at him. But now the shades were down, and it was *so* quiet. He pushed open the screen door and the whole second grade jumped out of the dining room, holding their presents for Jacob.

"Surprise! Surprise!" they screamed. They had big brown paper bags over their heads, with beaver faces painted on them.

His mother hugged him and the pitcher. His father picked up the cake from the dining table and showed it to Jacob. On top was a chocolate log with scratches on it for the bark. Peeking over the log, like

a little furry grandpa with a black cherry nose, was a beaver made out of sugar.

Everybody was talking to Jacob at the same time.

Gregory said, "Yesterday, I was so scared you were going to find out!"

"Every time you said 'beavers,' we started laughing," said Suzy.

"We couldn't help it," Katy said.

LaToya told him, "You are the smartest person about beavers we ever saw."

"You should be a beavers professor!" said LaTanya.

Honey said to Suzy, "Jacob looks like a cute little baby beaver, doesn't he?"

"You know what?" Franky poked Jacob. "Beavers aren't boring! They're the opposite. They're *un-boring!*"

Then he gave Jacob a beautiful birthday card from Margarita in Puerto Rico. It had purple shiny paper with gold letters. Inside, she had drawn a picture of a beaver. Franky read it for him: " '*Querido Jacob*' — that means 'Dear Jacob.' '*Feliz Cumpleaños*' — that means 'Happy Birthday.' '*Tu amiga*, Margarita' — that's 'Your friend, Margarita!'"

"Hey!" Jacob cried. "Let's eat my birthday cake! Except the beaver. That's for my beaver museum."

Suzy and Katy even loved their fairy wands. "This one is much better than the other kind because it has little stars that float up and down in the handle," they told Jacob. And Franky was figuring how he could make his pirate pencil sharpener shoot caps.

When Jacob blew out the candles, everybody sang:

"Happy beaver's day to you!
Happy beaver's day to you!
Happy beaver's day, dear Jacob.
Happy beaver's day to you!"

About the Author

Miriam Cohen draws on her own vivid memories of her childhood in Newburgh, New York, to help create her stories. She, her professor husband, and their three sons (who are all now grown) have lived all over the world in places as diverse as Texas, Afghanistan, and Brazil. Her family and travel have also inspired many stories. Like Jacob, Miriam Cohen's oldest son, Adam, loved beavers. "All of my three sons had fascinations like that," Ms. Cohen says. "Kids have a lovely way of becoming completely absorbed in something. And I wanted to pay tribute to that in *Second-Grade Friends*."

Ms. Cohen currently lives with her husband in Sunnyside, New York, where she loves to visit classrooms and observe the funny things kids say and do. That's why Jacob and his friends seem so real. They are.

Creepy, weird, wacky and funny things happen to the Bailey School Kids!™ Collect and read them all!

The Adventures of THE BAILEY SCHOOL KIDS®